THE BOXCAR CHILDREN®

THE YELLOW HOUSE MYSTERY

Time to Read™ is an early reader program designed to guide children to literacy success regardless of age or grade level. The program's three levels correspond to stages of reading readiness, making book selection straightforward, and assuring that when it's time for a child to read, the right book is waiting.

— Level — 1	**Beginning to Read**	• Large, simple type • Basic vocabulary	• Word repetition • Strong illustration support
— Level — 2	**Reading with Help**	• Short sentences • Engaging stories	• Simple dialogue • Illustration support
— Level — 3	**Reading Independently**	• Longer sentences • Harder words	• Short paragraphs • Increased story complexity

Library of Congress Cataloging-in-Publication data is on file with the publisher.

Printed in China
10 9 8 7 6 5 4 3 2 1 WKT 22 21 20 19 18

Cover and interior art by Shane Clester

Visit the Boxcar Children online at www.boxcarchildren.com.
For more information about Albert Whitman & Company,
visit our website at www.albertwhitman.com.

100 Years of Albert Whitman & Company
Celebrate with us in 2019!

THE BOXCAR CHILDREN®

THE YELLOW HOUSE MYSTERY

Based on the book by
Gertrude Chandler Warner

Albert Whitman & Company
Chicago, Illinois

"Grandfather, I have a question," said Benny Alden. "How come no one lives in the Yellow House?"

The Aldens were visiting
Surprise Island with Cousin Joe.
Henry, Jessie, Violet, and Benny
had explored the whole island.
But they had never been inside
the little house.
"That is an old story,"
said Grandfather.

"Many years ago, a man named
Bill lived here.
He built the Yellow House and
took care of the island."
"What happened to him?"
asked Jessie.

"That is the strange part,"
said Grandfather.
"He left the island one day
and did not come back.
No one knows where he went!"

"That *is* strange," said Henry.
"Did Bill take anything
with him?"
Grandfather sighed.
"Yes, you see, I had given him
some money to borrow."
"And he took it?" asked Violet.
"You must be mad!" said Benny.
"Oh, no," said Grandfather.
"It was many years ago.
I just hope Bill is okay,
wherever he is."

"Maybe we can find out
what happened," said Henry.
"Can we look for clues?"
"Of course," said Grandfather.
"But I do not think
there is anything to find."
The children looked all over.
But they did not find
a single clue.
Just like Grandfather said.
Until Benny noticed
something…

It was a secret hiding place!

There was a letter inside.

Bill, thank you for the money.

I can pay you back now.

Go to the little house you built on Bear Trail.

Look in the tin box.

"It sounds like Bill gave
the money to someone else,"
said Jessie.
"Maybe he left to get it back!"
"I've been to Bear Trail,"
said Joe.
"I used to hike there as a boy."
"Maybe we can find Bill!"
said Henry.
"Can we go and look,
Grandfather?"

"It has been many years since Bill left," said Grandfather. "But I guess a camping trip wouldn't hurt."

The children couldn't wait. A mystery and an adventure!

The next day, the children went
with Joe to Bear Trail.
They stopped at the trail store
for supplies.
The woman at the store did not
know Bill.
"You might find him at
Old Village," the woman said.
It would be a long trip.
But the Aldens did not mind.
They liked to explore.

Henry paddled with Violet.
Jessie paddled with Joe.
Benny was the lookout.

After a while, Benny saw
something.
"That tree is moving!" he said.
"That is no tree," laughed Joe.
"It's a moose!"
The animal swam right by
the canoes!

That night, the children
met a guide.
The guide did not know
Bill either.
But he did know about living
in the woods.
He taught Henry and Violet
to build a shelter.
Jessie and Benny cooked
supper over a campfire.

In the morning, the Aldens
reached the end of the lake.
"Are we done?" asked Benny.
"Not yet," said Henry.
"Old Village is on the next lake.
We need to hike."

The hike was hard work.
But Benny was happy
they weren't there yet.
He was having fun.

That night, the Aldens stayed
at a lumber camp.
One of the lumberjacks
was named Bill!
But he was too young.
The Bill they were looking for
would be older.

"We should reach Old Village tomorrow," said Joe. "We'll find the *real* Bill there." But things did not go as Joe planned…

The next day was windy
and gray.
Waves splashed the canoes.
It started to rain.
"Let's get to shore!" called Joe.

The wind blew harder.
The waves grew taller.
The Aldens made it to shore,
but Joe's canoe tipped over!

On land, Henry and Violet
made a shelter.
Jessie and Benny made
a campfire.

Soon, everyone was dry
and warm.
There was just one problem.
Their food was all wet!

Jessie had an idea.

"We can still cook the potatoes."

"And the milk is safe!"

said Henry.

It wasn't much.

But it was enough for the night.

"This isn't so bad," Benny said.

"We can call this Potato Camp!"

The next day was
clear and bright.
The children were hungry.
They could not wait
to get to Old Village.

When they arrived, an old man
greeted them.
The man was very kind.
He led them to a place to stay.

"Is this your little house?"
asked Violet.
The man nodded.
"I built it many years ago
for my hiking trips."

The children were happy for
a roof over their heads.
They were happy for food
on the table.
They were so happy, they forgot
to ask the old man's name!

"I like this place," said Benny.
"It's just like the Yellow House.
Except it's not yellow."
That gave Jessie an idea.
"Remember the letter we found?
It talked about a little house
on Bear Trail.
Maybe this is it!"

The children searched
the little house.
This time they did not
find any clues.

"The old man built this little house," said Jessie.
"And it is just like the Yellow House that Bill made."
"Do you think the old man is Bill?" asked Henry.

Suddenly, Benny called out.

"I found something!"

It was a tin box, just like
in the letter.

"This must be the right place!"
said Jessie.

"And that old man must be Bill!"
said Henry.

The Aldens went to the
old man.

"You're Bill!" said Benny.

"Why did you leave the Yellow
House?" asked Violet.

Bill explained.

"I gave your grandfather's
money to a friend.
He was going to pay me back.
But when I got here,
I could not find the money.
I felt so bad about losing it,
I was afraid to come home."

"Was the money in a tin box?"
asked Henry.
"Yes," said Bill.
"How did you know?"
The Aldens showed Bill
the box.
The money was still inside!

"You can come home now,"
said Violet.
"You don't think your
grandfather will be mad?"
Bill asked.
"No," said Violet.
"He just wants you to be safe."

Violet was right.
When Bill came home,
Grandfather was happy
to see him.

And with the money,
the Aldens helped Bill make…

a new start.

Keep reading with the Boxcar Children!

Henry, Jessie, Violet, and Benny used to live in a boxcar. Now they have adventures everywhere they go! What secrets will the children find on their very own island? Adapted from the feature film of the same name, this early reader allows kids to start reading with a Boxcar Children classic.

978-0-8075-7675-5 · US $12.99

GERTRUDE CHANDLER WARNER discovered when she was teaching that many readers who like an exciting story could find no books that were both easy and fun to read. She decided to try to meet this need, and her first book, *The Boxcar Children*, quickly proved she had succeeded.

Miss Warner drew on her own experiences to write the mystery. As a child she spent hours watching trains go by on the tracks opposite her family home. She often dreamed about what it would be like to set up housekeeping in a caboose or freight car—the situation the Alden children find themselves in.

While the mystery element is central to each of Miss Warner's books, she never thought of them as strictly juvenile mysteries. She liked to stress the Aldens' independence and resourcefulness and their solid New England devotion to using up and making do. The Aldens go about most of their adventures with as little adult supervision as possible—something else that delights young readers.

Miss Warner lived in Putnam, Connecticut, until her death in 1979. During her lifetime, she received hundreds of letters from girls and boys telling her how much they liked her books.